The Urbana Free Library

To renew: call **217-367-4057**
or go to **urbanafreelibrary.org**
and select **My Account**

Drawn
from
Nature

Helen Ahpornsiri

For my family, John, and little Helena
H. A.

Text and design copyright © 2018 by The Templar Company Limited
Illustrations copyright © 2018 by Helen Ahpornsiri
With thanks to Camilla de la Bédoyère, who consulted on this book

First U.S. edition 2018

Library of Congress Catalog Card Number pending
ISBN 978-0-7636-9898-0

17 18 19 20 21 22 TWP 10 9 8 7 6 5 4 3 2 1

Printed in Johor Bahru, Malaysia

This book was typeset in Garton and Perpetua and Aristelle script
The illustrations were created with petals and leaves.

BIG PICTURE PRESS
an imprint of
Candlewick Press
99 Dover Street
Somerville, Massachusetts 02144

www.candlewick.com

Drawn
from
Nature

Helen Ahpornsiri

B P P

Contents

SPRING

SUMMER

AUTUMN

WINTER

Introduction

Life in the wild doesn't stay still for long.
Year after year, plants bloom in spring and fade
in autumn in a cycle as old as time. Animals follow
the pattern of the seasons, too — searching for food and
rearing their young — sometimes roaming many miles
between one chapter of their lives and the next.

Each section of this book uncovers the season's
changes, brought to life with hand-pressed plants.
You can see spring in the pearly pink of a petal and
autumn in the fiery red of fallen leaves. You can see
leaves, stems, even berries, all woven into the images.
All you need to do is look beyond the surface. . . .

Spring

The winter frosts have melted and the long
nights are growing shorter – spring has finally
sprung. Snowdrops are the first flowers to rise,
leading the way for more bright buds and blossoms.
Chicks chirp in the trees, lambs frolic in the fields,
and tadpoles wriggle in the shallows. Everywhere
you look there is new life. It's just the beginning
of an incredible year in the wild.

The Spring Chorus

The start of spring means just one thing for most birds. It's time to find a mate.

In the hour before dawn, there is a flurry of birdsong: the dawn chorus is starting up. In this narrow window between night and day, birds call out to one another, hoping to get noticed. The fittest males have the best odds of attracting a female, as their song is the loudest and carries farthest.

As the sun rises higher in the sky, the birds then shift their attention to other matters. With more light to see by, it's time for them to go find breakfast. . . .

Blackbirds are one of the first birds to sing each morning.

Nest Building

Look carefully in spring and you may see busy birds with beaks full of twigs, grass, and moss – all the materials they need for nest building.

Once a nest is complete and the eggs are laid, parents take turns sitting on them until the first chicks appear. If everything goes according to plan, there will be plenty of food for the chicks by the time they hatch – and they don't take long to start demanding food. Many birds lay their eggs so they hatch just as the first juicy caterpillars appear. This clever timing means they'll never have far to fly to gather food for their young.

Small birds usually lay one egg a day until they have a full nest.

Nests are woven from twigs, then lined with soft moss or feathers.

The Trees Awake

After the long winter, trees are starting to show signs of change. Along their bare branches, tiny green buds appear, then slowly burst open, revealing the first new leaves of the year.

On other trees, you can see fluffy catkins – hanging clusters of flowers, whose pollen is carried in the wind. Their name comes from an old Dutch word for "kitten," because they look like furry cats' tails!

Meanwhile the leafy stems of young ferns stretch upward. Starting as tightly bound coils, their spiral shapes gradually open, unfurling to reveal a row of tiny fronds.

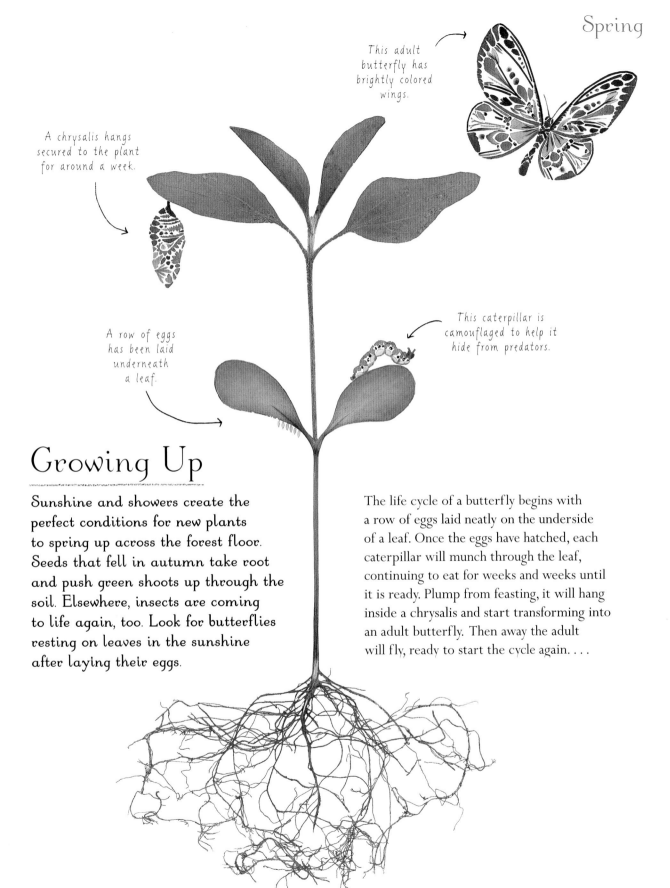

This adult butterfly has brightly colored wings.

A chrysalis hangs secured to the plant for around a week.

A row of eggs has been laid underneath a leaf.

This caterpillar is camouflaged to help it hide from predators.

Growing Up

Sunshine and showers create the perfect conditions for new plants to spring up across the forest floor. Seeds that fell in autumn take root and push green shoots up through the soil. Elsewhere, insects are coming to life again, too. Look for butterflies resting on leaves in the sunshine after laying their eggs.

The life cycle of a butterfly begins with a row of eggs laid neatly on the underside of a leaf. Once the eggs have hatched, each caterpillar will munch through the leaf, continuing to eat for weeks and weeks until it is ready. Plump from feasting, it will hang inside a chrysalis and start transforming into an adult butterfly. Then away the adult will fly, ready to start the cycle again. . . .

Hares Are Hopping

As the weather warms up, fields and meadows burst into life and hares can be seen darting through the long grass. Spotting a hare is a sure sign that spring has finally arrived.

This is the start of the hares' breeding season, when they can be seen "boxing" in the fields. Females stand on their rear legs and beat off males, who try to impress a potential partner with displays of their strength.

With their long, lean legs and muscular bodies, hares are incredibly fast runners. They spend their lives above ground, sleeping in grassy nests. Their young, called leverets, are able to run almost as soon as they are born.

Hares are larger than rabbits and can be identified by their long black-tipped ears.

Look for flattened patches of grass, which may show that a hare has been in the area.

Pond Life

Among the bulrushes at the edge of the pond, the water is teeming with activity.

Back at the start of spring, dozens of frogs arrived to mate and lay their eggs at the very pond where they were born. Now the jelly-like frog spawn is starting to hatch. Tiny black-headed tadpoles wriggle free, then swim away, looking for weeds to nibble on and seeking shelter from predators such as fish, newts, and insects. In a few weeks, they will grow legs and be ready to hop out of the water, just like their parents.

See if you can spot frog spawn, tadpoles, and hopping adult frogs in springtime ponds.

All in a Row

Out on the river, a line of fluffy ducklings follows their mother away from the bank and out across the rippling water.

Ducklings can swim almost as soon as they hatch, but their feathers are not quite waterproof yet. Until that moment comes, they must stay close to their mother, as her waterproof oil rubs off on their feathers and helps them stay afloat. Meanwhile, she keeps a watchful eye over her little ones.

Ducklings tend to swim in a long line, with the mother duck leading the way at the front.

"Blossom" is the name for the flowers of fruit trees, such as cherries, apples, and peaches.

Butterflies & Blossoms

A spring breeze blows, carrying with it a flurry of pink-white petals. They land, like snow, beneath the trees, where butterflies flit between banks of bright flowers.

The warm days of late spring tempt more and more butterflies to appear. Some have made long journeys on their migrations while others are just coming out of hibernation. The spring flowers provide a rich source of nectar for the butterflies — just what they need after the winter. You'll see them most on calm sunny days, when neither wind nor rain can threaten their delicate wings.

Butterflies enjoy visiting flowers such as bluebells, crocuses, and primroses.

Summer

As the year approaches its longest day, the weather gets hot and wildlife thrives. Crowds of insects are a welcome meal for birds as they arrive from their long migrations. Young families born in the spring are getting bigger, too, and you'll see them gradually venturing farther from home. All this activity is set against a colorful backdrop of flowers — a summer showstopper perfect for attracting bees.

In the Meadow

Out in the meadow, summer is in full swing — poppies sway in a gentle breeze, wheat turns golden in the sun, and nimble harvest mice climb the stalks in search of a midsummer feast.

Since the wheat is sown in spring, by summer it has grown tall and strong, and now its heads are heavy with grain. At summer's end, the crops will be harvested: the wheat grains will be ground into flour, and its stalks will be dried to make straw.

Although harvest mice like to nibble crops, they also help farmers by eating insect pests.

Each harvest mouse nest is about the size of an orange.

Harvest mice are the only species of mice to have prehensile tails, meaning they can be used for grasping onto stalks and stems.

In the midst of the field, harvest mice scurry up and down the wheat stalks. They are agile climbers, using their flexible tails like safety ropes as they run and leap. It's a long way down, but only up here will they find their favorite foods — berries, seeds, and tasty crops such as wheat and other grains.

Their neat, round nests are woven together from blades of grass and tucked up to three feet high, between tall plants. Here their tiny babies will be safe from most predators.

Swallows Swooping

Swifts and swallows fly with the seasons, following summer from place to place. Their fleeting visits are timed to make the most of the season's riches, as they gorge on all the insects they can catch.

At the start of summer, swifts and swallows arrive in the thousands, filling the skies as they pursue their prey of newly emerged insects. They are remarkably fast fliers, diving and turning in midair, sometimes flying just inches above the ground. When not in flight, they can often be seen perching together in a row along branches or power lines.

Swallows can fly for months at a time without landing.

Swallows can be differentiated from swifts or house martins by their long V-shaped tails.

Caterpillars can be seen munching on leaves all summer long.

Crickets have longer antennae than grasshoppers.

Crickets Chirping

On hot, muggy days, insects seem to be everywhere, and though they can't always be seen, you're sure to hear the sounds of crickets and grasshoppers chirping in the undergrowth.

These long-legged insects make their courtship calls by rubbing their legs and wings together – and they're not the only insects in search of a mate. After spending years underground as larvae, stag beetles reach maturity in summer and males start looking for a female. They will spend only a few weeks in their adult form, so there is no time to waste!

Male stag beetles have large antlers, which they use when fighting rival males.

With their bright bodies, dragonflies are easy to spot as they zip among the reeds.

In the Reeds

Along the water's edge, reed beds are full of activity. Flowers and grasses sway on their stalks, while ducks and moorhens hide their young families among the dense mass of stems.

Under the water's surface, the reeds also shelter young insects. Dragonfly larvae live underwater for up to two years, preying on tadpoles, fish, and other insects. On sunny days, the older larvae crawl out of the water and shed their skins, emerging as adults with colorful bodies and gauzy wings. The dragonflies must dry their wings in the sun before they can fly — but once they take to the air, they are one of the most formidable predators in the insect kingdom.

Irises and flowering grasses line riverbanks in summer.

Herons have long, sharp beaks for spearing fish.

Not only do reeds provide shelter; they also provide camouflage for hunters like herons. These lanky predators are perfectly suited to fishing in the shallows. They wade through the water on long legs, watching for fish with their keen yellow eyes. The moment they spot one, they'll strike out with lightning speed, using their long neck and sharp beak like a spear to stab the fish. Then they'll gulp it down all at once.

Leaves clockwise from
top: blackthorn, plane,
elder, Japanese maple,
black locust, field maple,
English oak

Glorious Green Leaves

Spring's pale new leaves have reached full size and deepened in color to a
rich, dark green. Where branches meet, they form a canopy above the forest
floor and cast dappled shade against the summer sun.

Leaves are the lungs of a tree: they are where air comes in and out of the plant and where
photosynthesis occurs — using energy from the sun to change carbon dioxide and water into
energy-rich sugars. For deciduous trees, which shed their leaves in autumn and grow new
ones in spring, summer is a time for growth and a chance to store up energy for winter.

Buds & Bees

Summer is the season for flowers, and everywhere you look, you'll see bright buds and buzzing bees.

The beautiful shapes, colors, and scents of flowers make them favorites with gardeners — but, even more important, these characteristics enable flowers to attract bees and other insects. Flowers depend on these visitors to carry pollen from plant to plant so that they can grow new seeds. In exchange, the insects are able to feed on the flowers' rich, sugary nectar.

Honeysuckle and bleeding heart flowers are known for their sweet nectar.

Bees buzz among forget-me-nots and violas.

Owls have wide, flat faces that act like satellite dishes directing tiny sounds toward their ears.

In some places, you can see fireflies on summer nights.

Summer Nights

As dusk settles into darkness, there are new faces to be seen: nocturnal animals that come out at night to look for their prey.

Humid evenings are perfect for hunting. Earthworms wriggle to the soil's surface, rodents scurry through the undergrowth, and the air is thick with flying insects – all ripe pickings for predators. Badgers and foxes, whose young are just old enough to fend for themselves, will eat whatever they can find, from beetles to birds. Owls swooping overhead are more particular, though. They glide silently, scanning the ground for a mouse to snatch up and carry away.

One badger can eat up to two hundred earthworms in a single night.

Autumn

The nights grow longer, the days grow cooler,
and the trees grow heavy with ripening fruit.
Food is still plentiful, but all the signs show that
winter is on its way. Animals hurry to make
their preparations, tending to their burrows and
gathering food for their stores. They must fatten up
before the cold season or else leave their summer
homes and make their way toward warmer lands.

Deer Rutting

As the sun rises and the autumn mists part, they reveal a great battle about to commence. It is the start of the annual deer rut, when males compete for the right to mate – and competition is fierce.

Two stags eye each other from a distance, turning their heads to the side to fully take in their opponent. Then, with perfect timing, the stags launch at each other, their bony antlers crashing together with a loud *crack*. Each rival aims to get to higher ground and knock the other male off balance.

It is a long, drawn-out fight and a dangerous undertaking. Ruts can result in injury and even death, but the risks are well worth it. The winner will become the dominant male in the herd and have his pick of mates. At the end of the battle, he bellows loudly to announce his victory. Defeated, the loser retreats into the mist. He will have to try his luck another time.

The "crack" of antlers clashing together can be heard from over a mile away.

The larger male will usually win.

Rutting stags often "crown" themselves with bracken to make themselves look more intimidating.

Deer shed their antlers after the rut and grow a new pair over the spring and summer.

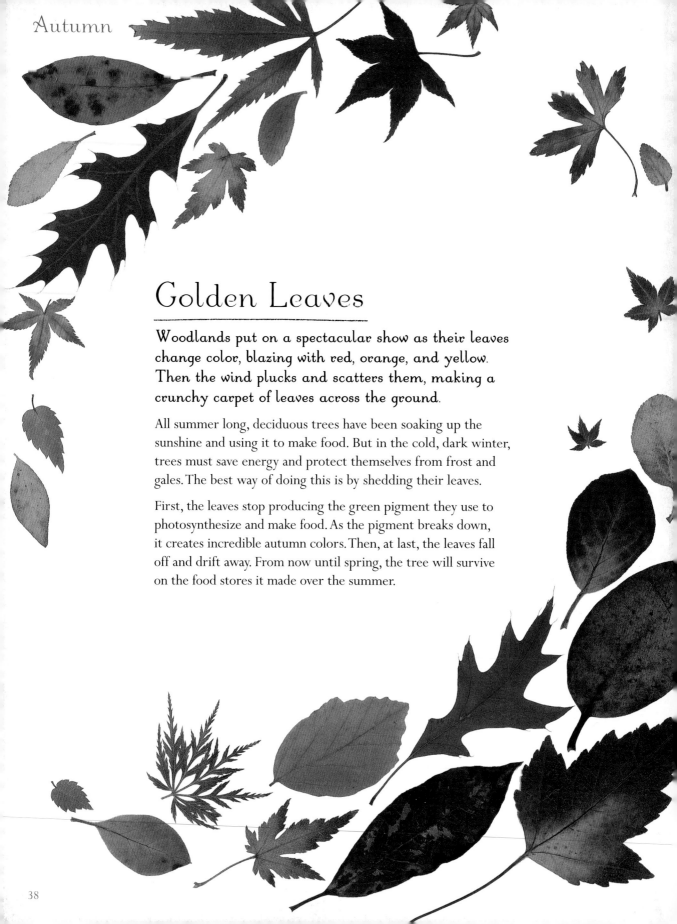

Golden Leaves

Woodlands put on a spectacular show as their leaves change color, blazing with red, orange, and yellow. Then the wind plucks and scatters them, making a crunchy carpet of leaves across the ground.

All summer long, deciduous trees have been soaking up the sunshine and using it to make food. But in the cold, dark winter, trees must save energy and protect themselves from frost and gales. The best way of doing this is by shedding their leaves.

First, the leaves stop producing the green pigment they use to photosynthesize and make food. As the pigment breaks down, it creates incredible autumn colors. Then, at last, the leaves fall off and drift away. From now until spring, the tree will survive on the food stores it made over the summer.

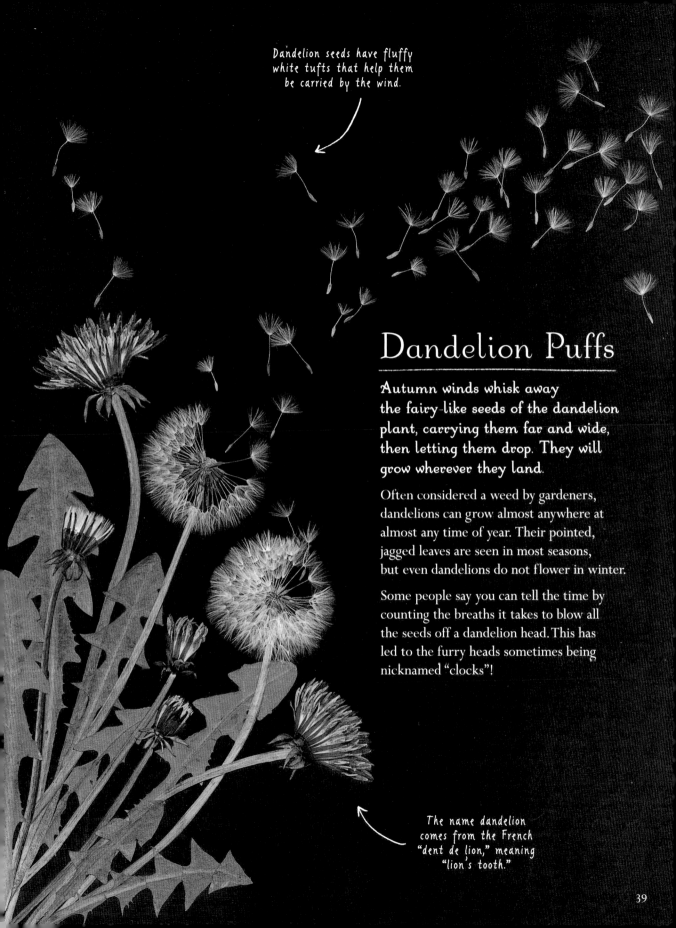

Dandelion seeds have fluffy
white tufts that help them
be carried by the wind.

Dandelion Puffs

Autumn winds whisk away
the fairy-like seeds of the dandelion
plant, carrying them far and wide,
then letting them drop. They will
grow wherever they land.

Often considered a weed by gardeners,
dandelions can grow almost anywhere at
almost any time of year. Their pointed,
jagged leaves are seen in most seasons,
but even dandelions do not flower in winter.

Some people say you can tell the time by
counting the breaths it takes to blow all
the seeds off a dandelion head. This has
led to the furry heads sometimes being
nicknamed "clocks"!

The name dandelion
comes from the French
"dent de lion," meaning
"lion's tooth."

Time to Fly

As temperatures drop and food becomes scarce, many animals undertake a long migration to warmer regions. Clouds of butterflies drift toward the equator, whales follow the coast, and some mammals start an epic overland trek. But perhaps the best-known migrators of all are birds.

The sounds of beating wings and echoing honks fill the skies as huge flocks leave their summer breeding grounds and head toward richer winter feeding grounds. Birds undertake some of the longest migrations in the animal kingdom, often following the same routes, known as flyways or migration corridors, for generation after generation.

You can see large birds such as ducks and geese flying in a distinctive V formation, which allows the birds at the back of the flock to save energy. When the bird at the front of the group grows tired, another will take its place.

Canada geese can be seen trailing across the sky in huge V formations.

Listen for noisy flocks of birds first thing in the morning and last thing before night.

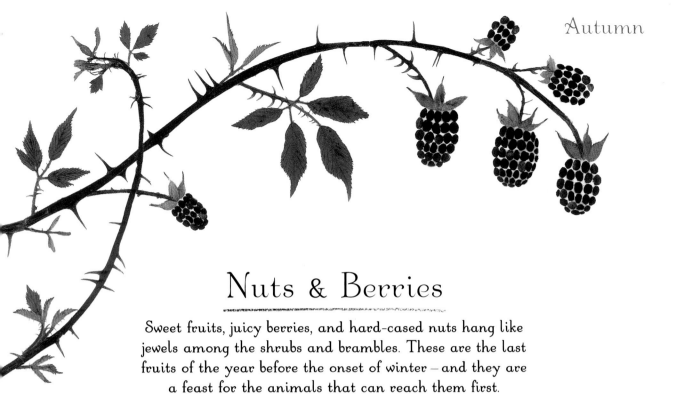

Nuts & Berries

Sweet fruits, juicy berries, and hard-cased nuts hang like jewels among the shrubs and brambles. These are the last fruits of the year before the onset of winter – and they are a feast for the animals that can reach them first.

Large animals such as deer and badgers gorge on fallen apples, while sharp-eyed birds peck the highest berries from the branches. Beneath the trees, bushy-tailed squirrels scamper back and forth as they do every year, gathering nuts for their winter stores and burying them in the ground so they can return for them during the hungry weeks ahead. Most nuts will be dug up before spring, but any that are lost or forgotten may one day grow into trees.

Horse chestnuts have a hard, spiky case to cushion their fall and protect them from animals.

43

Forest Fungi

Autumn is the best time of year to see mushrooms and other fungi as they burst up across the forest floor in incredible shapes and vibrant colors.

A mushroom or toadstool is only the aboveground part of a fungus. Most of it is hidden underground as a web of threads winding through the soil. When the heavy autumn rains fall, fungi spring up, revealing the part we call the fruit. Look for fungi around the trunks of trees, along the edges of fields, and growing in piles of autumn leaves.

While some fungi are safe to eat, many are poisonous. Only the most experienced experts can tell the difference between the two.

Never pick and eat wild mushrooms—
even if you think they look safe to eat.

Winter

Winter can be a hard time in the wild. It is cold
and dark, with frost and sometimes snow on the
ground. Animals are scarce, as many migrate or
hibernate and those that stay are tucked away
inside dens or nests. But look closely and you can
still see signs of life, from frosted spiderwebs to
paths of paw prints in the snow. Listen, too, and
you will hear birdsong, even in the depths of winter.

Bats hibernate upside down in their roosts.

Hibernation

For some animals, the only way to survive winter is to go into a long, deep sleep called hibernation. During this time, an animal does not eat, its body temperature drops, and its heart rate slows down, helping it to conserve energy.

Hibernating animals must eat as much as possible over the summer and autumn in order to build up their fat reserves. Then, as the weather gets colder, they will find somewhere safe to sleep: it needs to be sheltered from the worst of the winter weather and safe from predators. Small mammals such as mice and hedgehogs curl up in nests of leaves or burrows, while other animals look for shelter in caves, inside trees, or tucked away underneath piles of logs.

Frogs burrow underground or hide among piles of logs to hibernate.

Ladybugs crowd together under bark or in rock crevices.

A hibernating hedgehog's
heart rate drops from 190 beats
per minute to 20, and its
temperature falls to 50°F (10°C).

As leaves disintegrate, the fine networks of veins that carry water around them are revealed.

Bare Branches

The last of the leaves have been swept from the trees. Now their branches are still and bare, revealing their rough bark and twisting boughs – and sometimes even offering a glimpse of empty bird nests left over from spring.

While deciduous trees have lost their leaves, coniferous trees are still covered in green. Their thin needles or leaves have a waxy surface that prevents them from losing water and keeps them from freezing in even the coldest weather. So, with their needles or leaves intact, they can keep making food right through the season.

Cypress

Coniferous trees, sometimes known as evergreens, grow their seeds in spiky cones. Some have spiky needles, while others have scaly leaves.

Juniper

Larch

Douglas fir

Spruce

Grand fir

51

Birds of a Feather

Birds may have the option to take flight whenever they like, but winter is still a real test of their survival skills. Their main challenge is finding enough to eat, especially when snow and ice are covering the ground.

Many birds gather in groups, as huddling together provides warmth and they can increase their chances of finding food by spreading out and searching farther afield. With their thick layers of feathers, birds tend not to shiver from the cold, but you may notice some look particularly plump during winter. This is because they fluff air between their feathers to give them extra insulation.

Birds such as sparrows can be
seen perched together along
bare winter branches.

The smallest birds must eat
around 30 percent of their body
weight every day in order
to survive the winter.

Winter Berries

In the coldest weeks, evergreen plants such as holly and ivy still thrive. Their berries provide a welcome flash of color amid the wintry landscape.

Dense clumps of mistletoe hang high in the branches of other trees, where their pearly white berries are an attractive snack for passing birds. Other berries, like holly, are bright red, which makes them easy for birds to spot. Berries are one of the few food sources available for birds during winter, but the berries need the birds just as much as the birds need the berries. Their seeds are dispersed by being digested and then scattered in the birds' droppings.

Robins are easy to spot
with their bright-red
breast feathers.

Robin Redbreast

A chirrup of birdsong and a flicker of red reveal a robin hopping across the snowy ground. He has spotted a rival male, and there's not much that can stand in the way of this feisty little bird.

Most robins stay in the same place year-round for one simple reason: they are fiercely territorial birds and will defend their area from intruders at any cost. For the same reason, robins are also one of the only garden birds to sing all the way through winter. They use their song to mark their territory and scare away competition.

Birds will look for a high
perch to best show off their
colors and their song.

Red Fox at Night

On a cold, frosty night, a fox sets out, his paws crunching in the snow, his ears alert to the slightest sound of movement.

Although the ground is covered in a sheet of white, the fox can hear tiny sounds beneath the snow's surface and can pounce with great precision. His coat grows thicker in winter, and his bushy tail wraps around him like a blanket when he sleeps — keeping him snug on even the coldest nights.

When temperatures drop below freezing, water droplets freeze and turn to frost, coating everything in white.

A Note from the Artist

Everything you see in these pages — from the
gleam in a fox's eye to the delicate line of
a cobweb — is made from a plant.

Flowers and foliage are always changing with the seasons, but
here they have been paused in their life cycle, kindled with a new
story. Ferns have been transformed into feathers, and the colorful
wings of insects are formed from the very flowers they feed on.

Each collage is made from hundreds of leaves and flowers, which
are responsibly grown or foraged in the wild and preserved
with traditional flower-pressing methods. The plants are then
delicately arranged into bold new shapes and forms. They are all
brimming with the twists and tangles of the wilderness,
all capturing a perfect moment in time. . . .

H. Ahpornsiri

Glossary

camouflage: coloring that blends in with an animal's surroundings and helps it to hide

chrysalis: a hard case inside which a caterpillar changes into a butterfly

coniferous trees: trees that have needles all year round and produce their seeds in cones

deciduous trees: trees that shed their leaves in autumn and grow new ones in spring

fungus: an organism that grows and feeds on decaying matter; toadstools and mushrooms are both types of fungi

hibernation: a period of deep sleep some animals undergo to save energy and survive the winter

larva: a young insect before it develops into its adult form

migration: the movement of animals from one area to another, often following the seasons

nectar: A sugary liquid made by flowers and consumed by insects and other animals; bees use it to make honey

nocturnal: active at night

photosynthesis: the process by which green plants use the energy in sunlight to change carbon dioxide in the air and water from the soil into food for the plant to use